DOGNAPPED!

Written by
David J Robertson

Illustrated by ... Ward

Matador
9 Priory Business Park,
Wistow Road, Kibworth Beauchamp,
Leicestershire. LE8 0RX
Tel: 0116 279 2299
Email: books@troubador.co.uk
Web: www.troubador.co.uk/matador
Twitter: @matadorbooks

ISBN 978 1785891 441

British Library Cataloguing in Publication Data.
A catalogue record for this book is available from the British Library.

Printed and bound in Malta by Gutenberg Press Ltd.
Typeset in 13pt Gill Sans by Troubador Publishing Ltd, Leicester, UK

Matador is an imprint of Troubador Publishing Ltd

FOR KATE

CHAPTER ONE

THE BOAT

THUMP!

My eyes flew open beneath bushy brown eyebrows. My ears flicked to high alert.

'OW!'

I relaxed, the pained voice sounded very familiar.

Getting to my paws I shuffled forward and peered around the entrance to my kennel. One-Eyed Rose sat outside, pulling a face as she rubbed her head.

'Wow! Hello Misty,' she winced, 'I bashed into your house.'

'I suppose you were running around sniffing at this and sniffing at that…'

'Not looking where I was going!' she interrupted.

'…as usual,' I continued. One-Eyed Rose always runs around sniffing at this and that.

She stood up a little unsteadily, her shaggy spaniel ears dragging on the ground.

'Are you alright?' I asked. But One-Eyed Rose is never anything else.

She wagged her tail enthusiastically as though nothing had happened, although a big lump had appeared through the scruffy brown fur on top of her head.

'So what shall we do today?' One-Eyed Rose looked at me through her one good eye.

She had been squashed by the school bus when she was a puppy. Even then she never looked where she was going. The vet people fixed her really well, but they couldn't mend her eye, so now she bumps into things a lot.

'Perhaps we should try to find Bertie,' I replied. Bertie is one of our friends. 'He was going for a walk along the canal.'

'Wow! I like the canal, there are plenty of things to sniff.' One-Eyed Rose scampered off to find Bertie.

I stretched out my front legs, white socked paws flat along the ground. I arched my back and shifted forward to stretch my hind legs.

I shook myself from head to bushy tail so my shiny black and white fur fell back neatly. We Border collies arc very particular about our appearance.

Smoothing out my bib I licked a stubborn tuft of fur into place and ambled off after my dizzy friend.

Bertie sat on the tow path. One-Eyed Rose stood beside him. Both had their heads tilted to one side, concentrating hard as they stared at a narrow-boat which was moored alongside. The boat was coloured in shades of blue with lots of windows along the sides.

'Hi guys, what's happening?' I asked as I got nearer.

'Wow! You'll never guess, Misty,' One-Eyed Rose ran around in excited circles.

'Guess what?'

One-Eyed Rose looked puzzled, 'I'm not sure. You'd better ask Bertie.'

Bertie is a small brown terrier. He is always smartly dressed with a bone-patterned scarf instead of a collar. Bertie is very old, so he knows a lot of things about a lot of things. He looked deep in thought as he stroked his long grey whiskers.

'OOOOwwww!'

I jumped at the noise coming from the boat, my fur standing on end.

'Wow!' One-Eyed Rose stood still for a second, 'It happened again!'

Bertie turned to look at me, 'That noise keeps coming from the chimney,' he pointed a paw at a long black tube sticking from the roof.

'It's very scary!' shouted One-Eyed Rose, 'Let's go and see what it is.'

'Be careful, Rose,' I warned her.

Our friend wasn't easily frightened. She scurried to the boat and tried to jump onto the roof. She failed at the first attempt; and the second. After the third clumsy landing, she lay panting on the grassy bank. 'It's too high,' she complained.

Bertie considered the problem. 'You need something to stand on,' he announced.

I grimaced as One-Eyed Rose stuck her paw in my ear. She squashed my nose as she tried to balance on my back. 'It's still too high,' she shouted, jumping up and down trying to scramble onto the roof.

'Rose, you're messing up my fur!' I grunted as she landed on top of me again.

Bertie stroked his long grey whiskers harder, 'You need something taller; where's Rascal?'

One-Eyed Rose tumbled to the ground, 'I haven't seen him.'

'Nor me,' I shrugged.

'He was here not long ago,' Bertie peered along the towpath. 'Just before that noise started.'

'OOoowww!' moaned the chimney.

CHAPTER TWO

TICKLING

Bertie and I exchanged knowing looks. Rascal is a huge German shepherd with paws as big as my dinner bowl. He looks fierce, but Rascal is scared of his own shadow.

'He's hiding!' we said together.

'Let me find him,' our sniffing friend set off, tail wagging crazily. She sniffed at this and that until she stopped in front of a tree pointing her nose.

Two large trembling ears stuck out either side of the trunk.

'OOOWWW!' went the boat.

'Oooh!' moaned Rascal softly.

'Rascal, we need to stand on your back,' I looked around the tree at the giant who sat shaking with his front paws over his eyes.

'Noooo!'

Bertie ambled over, 'Rascal, we need your help.'

'It sounds scary! I'm stopping here!'

One-Eyed Rose pushed her paws deep into his long thick fur and shoved with all her might. Rascal didn't budge.

'OOOOwwww!'

'OOOh!'

Rascal trembled.

Bertie stroked his long grey whiskers, thinking once more.

I sat with One-Eyed Rose on the bank and watched the chimney, both of us cocking our

heads every time it made a noise, trying to understand what was going on.

'Got it!' Bertie shouted. 'I've had a big idea.'

Bertie is good at big ideas. He has big ideas a lot.

He wandered across to whisper into my furry ear.

I nodded.

I lifted One-Eyed Rose's long floppy ear and repeated Bertie's big idea.

'Wow!' she smoothed her ear back into place, 'We're going to pickle Rascal! Why?'

'Ssssh!' we shushed. 'We don't want Rascal to hear and run away.'

I whispered to her again, making sure that she heard properly this time.

'Oh!' said One-Eyed Rose rather too loudly, 'I think I understand.'

Bertie smiled at Rascal as he rounded the tree trunk. 'How are things?'

Rascal looked at him suspiciously. I got into position while his attention was distracted.

One-Eyed Rose whistled innocently as she approached from the other side.

'Go!' shouted Bertie.

I jumped forward and began to tickle Rascal's tummy.

'Ohhh! Nooo! Ha ha. He hee,' he leapt to his feet.

One-Eyed Rose grunted as she pushed from the back.

Bertie panted as he steered from the front.

Rascal unwillingly edged forward.

'Nooo! Ha he. He ha.'

Tickle.

Push.

Pant.

'Ha. Noo! He.'

Steer.

Grunt.

Tickle.

Rascal shook through fear and ticklement, but we coaxed him alongside the boat.

'Now!' puffed Bertie, out of breath.

I hurried out from beneath the long legs and leapt onto Rascal's back. One-Eyed Rose followed, scampered up my bushy tail, clambered onto my back and leapt for the roof.

Her paws flailed, trying to get a grip.

She began to slip backward.

'OOOwww!' howled the chimney.

Rascal shot off in terror tripping over the mooring rope as he went, tearing it loose.

I briefly hung in mid-air.

One-Eyed Rose made one last lunge.

I tumbled, landing hard on my tail bone.

The spaniel dangled from the boat. Slowly she hauled herself up.

I rubbed my sore tail. Bertie had disappeared and I could see Rascal's quivering ears sticking out from both sides of the tree trunk again.

'Wow! That was fun!' One-Eyed Rose called from somewhere above me.

'OOOwww!' went the chimney.

I looked up. One-Eyed Rose already had her one good eye peering down the tube.

'There's something stuck in here,' she called.

'Perhaps you'd better not disturb it, Rose,' I shouted.

One-Eyed Rose tore out of sight across the roof, 'I need a stick.'

'Ooooww!'

The spaniel reappeared carrying a broom in her mouth. She twisted her head and plunged the handle into the narrow vent.

'OWWWW!' from the chimney.

One-Eyed Rose pushed again.

'OOOOOW!'

THWUP! A puff of soot shot out of the pipe

There was a loud THUMP somewhere inside the boat. The broom handle clattered down the chimney and sat with the brush rocking on the rim.

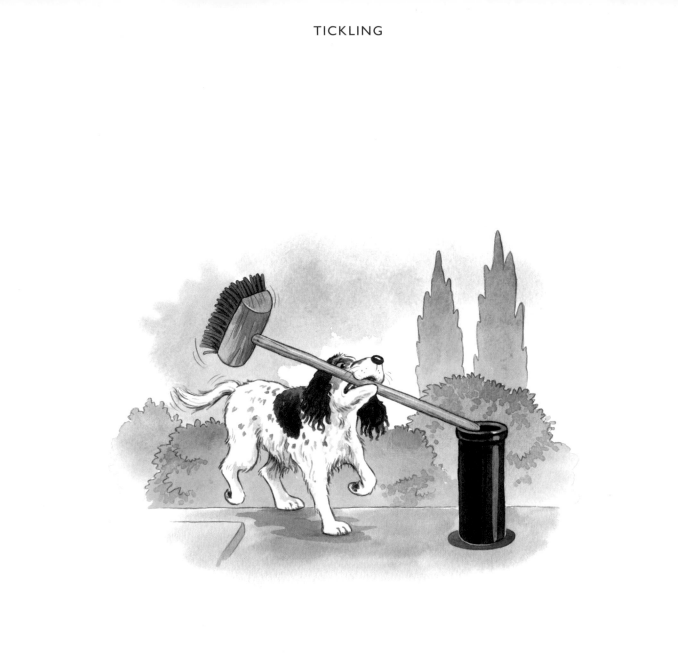

CHAPTER THREE

ASHLEY

One-Eyed Rose peered once more into the chimney. 'Wow! It's gone – whatever it was!' she exclaimed, standing back. Now her one good eye had a black sooty ring around it.

I leant my paws against the window and put my nose to the glass. Inside were two black lumps. One was vaguely Bertie shaped. The other was a lot smaller.

The largest lump shook violently. Soot billowed through the air. It was Bertie! He blinked at me through the glass and pointed toward the back of the boat as he shouted, 'The door was open all the time.'

I scurried along the bank and sprang onto the tiny deck. Clouds of black dust hung around the open door. Carefully, I made my way down three narrow steps and peered into the gloomy cabin.

Bertie stroked his long black whiskers which were slowly becoming grey again. In front of him the small black lump trembled. Two vivid white circles appeared.

The lump had eyes!

I took a step back. This was getting scarier. Even Bertie, who knows a lot of things about a lot of things looked worried.

Looking round I spotted a carving knife lying on a table. I picked it up in my jaws – just in case!

'Ahh…!' went the tiny black lump.

It trembled harder than before.

…AAh!'

And even harder.

'Is everything all right?' One-Eyed Rose yelled down the chimney.

'…Tishoooo!' sneezed the tiny black lump, showering more soot into the air.

'Wow! What was that?' boomed from the chimney. 'Hold on I'm coming down.'

The tiny lump puffed out its cheeks. 'Tshoo,' it sniffed. It was now mostly white with brown patches and a brown tipped stubby tail.

Scamper!

Clatter!

Bang!

Thump!

One-Eyed Rose fell down the steps, 'Wow! A puppy dog!'

The pup looked at Bertie with his bone-patterned scarf. He stared at me armed with a knife. Finally he gaped at One-Eyed Rose with the black ring around her one good eye like an eye-patch. 'Arggh! Pirates!'

'Wow! Where?' shouted One-Eyed Rose, looking around anxiously.

I dropped the knife. 'He means us, Rose,' I told her, 'we've frightened him.'

The pup bounced up and down on all four paws. 'I'm not frightened! Come on! I'll fight you all. Yippity yap!' he barked in a squeaky voice.

Bertie sighed. With a sharp clip of his paw he tapped the puppy across the tail making him somersault backwards.

'Ow! I surrender!'

'What sort of dog is that?' One-Eyed Rose sniffed at the defeated baby.

'I won't tell you anything! We Jack Russells are very brave!'

I looked at the brown marks on his fur, 'I bet his name is Patch.'

The little dog grinned at me defiantly, 'You'll get nothing out of me, you nasty pirate. From now on Ashley says nothing! Yappity yip!'

'So, Ashley, what was a Jack Russell puppy doing up the chimney?' Bertie asked.

Ashley pouted, 'I was exploring.'

'It's a good job I poked you out with that brush. If someone had lit the fire you might have singed your tail,' One-Eyed Rose said helpfully.

Something felt wrong. Glancing up I noticed a tree moving slowly past the window. 'Er, guys…'

Bertie and One-Eyed Rose were examining Ashley. They ignored me.

'…guys…' Another tree went by, slightly faster.

'…we're moving!' I shot out of the cabin, onto the deck. The mooring rope skittered along the towpath as we drifted away.

'Wow! What do we do now?' One-Eyed Rose had clambered up beside me.

'Help! I'm being dognapped!' Ashley yapped.

'I've had another big idea,' Bertie announced, shouting, 'Rascal!'

Rascal peered around his hidey tree as we wallowed along.

'Grab the rope,' Bertie pointed with his paw.

Rascal hesitated for a moment, but even a big furry coward could not leave his friends in trouble. He galloped forward.

'Oh no!' Ashley sighed, 'Another one; my goodness, isn't he big!'

Rascal grabbed the rope in his massive jaws and dug his paws into the bank.

The boat was too strong.

Rascal skidded along behind, straining for all he was worth.

'Come on, Rascal,' we shouted encouragement.

Rascal dug his paws in deeper.

'I hope you fall in the water, you baddy,' shouted Ashley. 'Yippity, yip, yap!'

Rascal ploughed four furrows into the grass.

The boat slowed.

We cheered.

Ashley booed.

Rascal caught his front paws in the soft ground.

'Yippity, yappity. Yip!'

Rascal's front legs stopped; unfortunately his tail end didn't.

'Aaaagh!' Rascal catapulted through the air.

He dropped the rope.

'Wow! Rascal can fly,' One-Eyed Rose watched in wonder as our friend sailed overhead.

SPLAAADOING!

Rascal landed hard on the metal roof.

I winced; that must have hurt.

'Hah!' Ashley clapped his paws together, 'One down, three to go!'

Ashley bounced off my back and sprang onto the roof. He stood on poor Rascal's back, 'Ashley the pirate slayer!' he cheered.

Rascal groaned as he tried to stand, dislodging the puppy.

Ashley flipped over, 'Ow!'

Stunned, Rascal fell off the roof, crashed down the stairs and disappeared into the cabin.

'Rats!' muttered Ashley, 'I thought he was dead!'

CHAPTER FOUR

THE BUTTON

Helplessly we drifted along.

Bertie went to make sure Rascal was alright.

'Yippity yap!' Ashley scolded from the roof.

One-Eyed Rose examined a big green button with the letters,

START

on a label underneath. 'What does this say?'

'I can't read, Rose,' I sighed.

'I know what it says,' Ashley peered over the edge of the roof.

'What! Don't tell me you can read,' I glared at the puppy.

"Dognappers are in *big* trouble." Ashley sniggered, 'That's what it says.'

One-Eyed Rose lifted her paw to press it. 'Let's see what happens.'

'Rose! No!' but I was too late.

From somewhere beneath our paws something rumbled.

Then spluttered.

It chugged.

Then – chug, splutter, chug, CHUG CHUG CHUG.

'Rose, you started the engine!' I shouted.

'*Big* trouble!' Ashley hooted.

One-Eyed Rose nudged a lever with her nose, 'Perhaps this stops it.'

The craft shot forward.

BASH! It crashed into the bank, bounced off and headed for the other side.

BOING!

We zigged and zagged across the canal.

Zig. CRASH!

Zag. BANG!

Zig. WALLOP!

'Use the tiller to steer,' Ashley howled with laughter.

'The what?'

'That big stick behind you.'

I leaned on the handle, 'Which way?'

Ashley rolled his eyes, 'I'm only a puppy dog. Do you expect me to know everything!'

I pushed left with all my might. The boat went right.

SMASH!

'Go the other way!' One-Eyed Rose shouted.

I steered right. The boat went left.

SPLAT!

'Not so hard!' Bertie had reappeared to see what the noise was about.

I pushed gently. The boat straightened. We chugged down the middle of the water.

'Are we sinking?' Rascal's trembling voice echoed up the stair. 'I can't swim.'

Peering into the cabin I saw the terrified chump shaking like jelly. He looked silly.

'Rascal, you look silly,' One-Eyed Rose called down.

'At least I won't drown!' Rascal wore a big yellow sou'wester hat, an enormous oilskin coat with an orange life jacket underneath. He had four welly boots, all on the wrong paws because they stuck out at odd angles. 'I found these in a cupboard.'

'You're not very good pirates,' Ashley shook his head sadly. 'Frankly I'm a bit disappointed.'

CHAPTER FIVE

THE LOCK

'How do we stop?' I asked Bertie.

'Perhaps we ought to press something else to see what happens,' Bertie stroked his long grey whiskers as he studied the controls.

'Are you sure?' but I was too late as Bertie stabbed at a button.

'*And finally ,*' said the radio, ' *a poor baby elephant has been washed off the deck of his boat as he was going to the zoo and is lost at sea.*'

'Wow!' One-Eyed Rose was back again, 'Perhaps we'll see him.' She peered over the side of the boat with her bottom in the air and her tail wagging furiously to see if she could see the elephant.

'Rose, we're a long way from the sea,' Bertie switched off the radio again. 'The sea is all the way over by America, just past London.'

'That's just as well,' One-Eyed Rose set off for the front end again. 'I don't know what an elephant looks like,' she called over her shoulder.

We floated along. I was used to the steering now.

One-Eyed Rose kept coming back with news from the front end.

Bertie pulled at his long grey whiskers, thinking of big ideas.

Rascal was hiding somewhere below.

Ashley had worn himself out and was dozing quietly.

'Erm…' One-Eyed Rose wandered back slowly. '…I think we're in trouble.'

'What sort of trouble?' Bertie looked worried.

'There's something in the way.'

Ashley woke and lifted a tiny ear. From his position on the roof he looked out across the water. 'Ha! It's a lock, I can see the gates.'

'Gates?' my voice quavered.

'A lock makes the boat go up or down inside two sets of gates,' advised the young sailor, 'now you're in real trouble!'

Fortunately the front gates of the lock were open. We sped past them.

Unfortunately this meant that the back gates were shut.

The boat rammed them.

Hard!

People stood around the lock. They laughed and pointed when they saw us. 'Look at those funny dogs on that boat!'

'Isn't that little one on the roof cute.'

'Help, I'm being dognapped!' Ashley shouted.

'Yippety yappity yip,' heard the people.

'Never mind, we can help,' they shouted as they began to turn handles and pull levers.

The gates behind us closed.

'Yap, yip, yappity,' Ashley told them.

The water began to drain away and we were lowered down into the lock.

'Oh no! We're sinking,' Rascal moaned from somewhere inside.

It began to get very dark as we descended lower and lower.

One-Eyed Rose looked up, 'Wow! The sky is getting smaller!'

Bertie gulped.

I clung onto the tiller for all I was worth.

Ashley giggled at the sight of so many scaredy pirates.

Just as I thought that we could get no lower the gates opened and the boat surged forward.

'Goodbye,' waved the people, 'glad we could help. Enjoy your trip.'

CHAPTER SIX

THE WEIR

We sailed on through the afternoon. The sun shone and ducks quacked. I was beginning to enjoy myself.

Rascal had still not reappeared.

Ashley went into the cabin to sulk about being dognapped.

Now and then I listened to the radio to see what was happening.

'*News is coming in of a dognapping. Young Ashley has been taken along with a narrow-boat. His people are very upset. In a statement they said, 'Whoever has taken our poor puppy is very naughty indeed.'*'

Bertie looked at me and shook his head sadly, 'Now we are in *big* trouble.'

'*…and nobody has found the baby elephant yet,*' continued the radio.

I showed One-Eyed Rose how to steer the boat and if she stretched as high as possible she could just reach the tiller. At least I could have a rest. I curled my bushy black tail over my nose and tried to sleep.

'Wow! What's this?' One-Eyed Rose woke me almost immediately.

I opened an eye to see a sign on the bank. It had letters with,

CANAL THIS WAY

and an arrow pointing left.

Another arrow pointed right with,

DANGER! WEIR

and underneath in smaller letters,

I WOULDN'T GO THIS WAY IF I WERE YOU!

One-Eyed Rose shrugged, 'I wonder what that said?'
As I opened my mouth to answer the boat sped up, 'Rose, what have you done!'
'I didn't touch anything. I was only steering like you showed me.'
We began moving faster.
And faster.
'Rose! What's happening?' Bertie and Ashley dashed onto the deck.
One-Eyed Rose was tossed about as she tried to hang onto the tiller. I grabbed hold trying to help but now we were both flung from side to side. Bertie grabbed my legs to hold me down and was swished across the deck.
'What's happening?' I shouted.
Ashley pointed left. 'The canal went that way.'
'Where are we going?' Bertie swished back the other way.
'I don't know, but I think we might all die, you nasty puppy murdering pirates!'
SCCCRAAAPPPE!
The bottom of the boat caught on something and squealed as it stopped.
We were flung to the floor.
'Thank goodness we're safe,' someone muttered next to my ear.
The eerie silence was only broken by the sound of Rascal sobbing somewhere below.
Cautiously I untangled myself.
One-Eyed Rose fidgeted as usual.
Bertie hauled himself up.

Ashley scratched an ear with his hind paw. 'At least we've stopped! Are you going to let me go now?'

SCCRRREECH!

The front end dipped, the boat slid forward. The deck rose sharply, tangling us up.

WHAWHAWHAWHAWHA.

The propeller was out of the water, churning fresh air.

'Aaaagh!' Rascal screamed.

'Wow!' shouted One-Eyed Rose.

'Get off my whiskers!' demanded Bertie.

'Ship wreckers!' yipped Ashley.

'Everybody stay calm,' I tried to reassure them.

Up went the front end.

The back splashed down, soaking us.

The propeller caught the water and shot us forward.

CRUNCH!

The boat pitched over.

Ashley slid across the deck.

Bertie grabbed his tail.

One-Eyed Rose clung to Bertie.

Gritting my teeth I grabbed the spaniel's leg and hooked a paw around the door frame.

GRIND!

Ashley slid back as the boat pitched again.

Our chain of dogs followed.

My grip weakened.

SPLASH!

'Yippity yap!' Ashley squealed.

I was tiring fast, 'I can't hold on!'

We struck rocks, but the boat was moving so fast it bounced over them.

The next wave was the final straw.

I let go.

We slid toward the back.

'Dogs overboard!' I shouted.

A terrible pain shot through my tail.

Still I held One-Eyed Rose, who was stretched full length gripping Bertie.

Ashley dangled over the side, with Bertie pulling him for all he was worth.

We were dragged back to safety as the ache in my tail worsened.

Rascal unclamped his enormous jaws from my rear end and dumped us onto the deck.

'Sorry, Misty, it was all I could do,' he muttered.

'At least we're safe,' I grimaced.

'Look out!' Rascal warned.

'Rose. No!' Bertie shouted.

I looked around to see a terrifying sight.

One-Eyed Rose tensed her body and twisted one way and then the other. She shook violently from head to tail, showering us with water once more.

'Thanks Rose!' I dribbled.

'Wow! That was fun. We should do it again sometime,' grinned my soggy friend.

CHAPTER SEVEN

THE SEA MONSTER

Evening came. The boat was moving a lot faster, the water pushed us along while the engine chugged away showing no sign of stopping.

'I think we're on a river,' said Bertie, thoughtfully stroking his long grey whiskers.

One-Eyed Rose dashed backward and forward even more, excited by the new turn of events. Rascal had disappeared below, although we occasionally heard him sobbing.

'Guess where rivers go to,' Ashley was giggling again.

'Where?' I wasn't sure I really wanted to know.

'To the sea!' said Bertie, grimly.

'Now we might find that elephant,' One-Eyed Rose appeared briefly, before scampering off again. 'I'll tell Rascal where we're going,' she called back.

I looked around anxiously. Through the gathering darkness the river-banks seemed a long way away and we were now passing much larger boats moored up on either side. No one seemed to notice us as we slipped past.

We watched as the lights of an enormous city lit up the banks on either side. We chugged under bridges heavy with traffic, but everyone was too busy to see our little boat passing below. Still we sailed on. Daybreak came and went. The river got wider.

Eventually we passed a tall white tower. 'That's a lighthouse,' said Ashley, but he wasn't laughing now. 'We're at sea.'

The boat was bobbing up and down in the waves. Some of the sea splashed into the boat. It began to rain. And then at last, but too late, the engine cut out.

We were adrift!

Bertie, Ashley, One-Eyed Rose and I huddled together, too scared to say what we really thought, until, 'WE'RE ALL GOING TO DROWN!' Rascal shot up from below. 'My paws are wet, the boat's filling with water!'

Again we made a chain of dogs, this time passing welly boots between us. Rascal filled one with water and passed it to One-Eyed Rose on the steps. She handed it to me out on deck. I passed it to Bertie who emptied it over the side. Ashley grabbed the empty boot and tossed it back into the cabin for Rascal to refill.

'It's getting deeper!' Rascal howled.

'Bale faster!' yelled One-Eyed Rose.

'Pass faster!' I shouted.

'The wind is blowing water back on board,' dribbled Bertie, soaking wet and pouring for all he was worth.

'Mmmmmph!' said Ashley mouth full of welly boot.

'*Barrooo!*' I heard in the distance.

'What was that?' I asked, cocking an ear.

'*Barroo!*' I heard again.

'Can anyone else hear that?' I swivelled both ears in the direction of the noise.

'*Barroo!*'

'QUIET!' I shouted.

We listened. Rain pelted onto the roof. The wind howled. Waves crashed against the boat pitching it violently back and forth.

'*BARROO!*'

'Look,' said Ashley, 'there's something floating toward us.'

'Wow!' One-Eyed Rose had the best view. 'It's a square boat with a grey chimney and we're going to...'

CRUNCH! *'BARROO!'*

'...hit it!'

Planks of wood floated past. 'It must have been a packing case.' said Bertie.

A grey tentacle snaked past my nose.

'Aargh! A sea monster.' squealed Rascal.

The tentacle pulled on the tiller and a large grey head appeared over the side of the boat.

'That's a trunk,' shouted Bertie, 'it's the baby elephant. Help it. Quick.'

I pulled one ear while One-Eyed Rose tugged the other. Rascal used his enormous strength to haul on the trunk. The elephant flopped onto the deck. 'Barroo?' it went.

'Wow!' for once One-Eyed Rose had nothing more to say.

'So what now?' Rascal trembled. 'We're sinking even faster with this great lump on board.'

Bertie stroked his long grey whiskers, wondering what to do.

'Does anyone speak elephant?' I asked.

Ashley was miming the doggy paddle. Rascal tried to imitate someone drowning. Me and Bertie pretended to row the boat while One-Eyed Rose for some reason mimicked the back stroke. The elephant looked happy to be safe but seemed very confused, it looked at each of us in turn.

Its eyes lit up, 'Barroo,' it seemed to have got the

message that we were in trouble. The trunk grabbed Ashley and curled him toward the elephant's mouth.

'Oh no! It's going to eat Ashley,' Rascal quavered.

'Might not be such a bad idea,' shrugged One-Eyed Rose, 'I'm a bit hungry myself.'

But the elephant gave the little dog a big sloppy kiss, lowered him back and dropped its trunk into the rising water.

It took a deep breath and sucked. The trunk, now full of water, lifted over the back of the boat.

The elephant blew.

Water powered out.

The boat shot forward like it was jet propelled.

The elephant lowered its trunk into the flooded cabin again.

'Let me grab the tiller!' I shouted, 'I'll steer us back to land.

CHAPTER EIGHT

BORIS

The elephant squirted us toward the river we'd left earlier. As we got closer to land we heard a noise which got louder and louder. We saw people standing along the river bank, yelling and waving their arms.

Boats surged toward us, some with sirens and flashing blue lights while others sprayed water high into the air. All of them were full of people shouting so loud that we couldn't make out what any of them were saying.

'Now we're in trouble,' Rascal tried to make himself as small as possible, not easy for such a big dog, 'that must be all the people in the whole wide world!'

'They'll send you to prison,' Ashley was giggling once more.

'What's prison?' One-Eyed Rose wanted to know.

Bertie explained about prison and One-Eyed Rose decided that she might not like it very much.

'I can't steer properly. All these boats are squeezing us into the bank,' I said.

SPLAAANG! We slammed into a jetty and shuddered to a halt.

All the people in the whole wide world surged toward us.

'STOP!' The crowds parted and a man who looked very important pushed through the throng. 'Hello,' he said, 'my name is Boris and I'm the Mayor of all the people.'

Ashley shouted, 'I've been dognapped by these baddies and they should all be put into prison until teatime at least!'

Boris laughed and patted Ashley's head, 'It's a shame you can't talk and tell us what went on as you rescued this poor baby elephant.'

'Yippety yap,' Ashley tried again.

'Barroo!' trumpeted the elephant on hearing its name. The people cheered. Boris waved his arms up and down to quiet them.

'What brave dogs! You are heroes. I have a medal for Ashley and the finest sausages for everyone else.'

'Heroes? Well of course, as it was my boat and my idea I think I should take most of the credit,' Ashley yapped away. 'I only asked the others along to help get the elephant on board. He is a bit heavy and I am only a puppy after all.'

We left Ashley to take the applause, now sitting astride the elephant, saluting, waving and posing for photographs.

The rest of us wolfed down platefuls of sausages.

As I was eating I thought of a big problem I wiped my mouth, 'How are we getting home?' I asked.

Bertie stroked his long grey whiskers.

One-Eyed Rose sniffed at her plate.

Rascal trembled.

'Not by boat!' they chorused.

COMING SOON

THE NEXT MISTY BOOK —

IN THE DOGHOUSE

www.mistybooks.net